Unravelin the Riddle

By

Christina Abby

This book is a work of fiction. Places, events, and situations in this story are purely fictional. Any resemblance to actual persons, living or dead, is coincidental.

ISBN: 1-4033-5086-8 (E-book)
ISBN: 1-4033-5087-6 (Paperback)
ISBN: 1-4107-0665-6 (Dustjacket)

This book is printed on acid free paper.

1stBooks - rev. 02/15/03

ACKNOWLEDGMENTS

Thanks to my siblings: Bettie J. Williams, Idella Taylor, Conney Abby, Dorothy Walker, and Charline Broom for being who they are.

Thanks to all my folk in Clarksdale, Mississippi, whose amazing faith, like individual starbursts, tastefully captivate and titillate the core of my soul. Thanks to my former coworkers in Fulton County's Human Services Department, Atlanta, Georgia. More specifically, the Yellow Team members who unmistakably bring the light: Melodic Mclinda, Breathtaking Brigitte, Beautiful Barbara, Resourceful Robin, Demonstrative David, Dedicated Damon, Willing Willie, Gorgeous George, Cool Carlos, Precocious Portia, Sensational Sonia, Jazzy James, Benevolent Beatrice, Magnificent Monica, Gracious Gerry, Terrific Tanga, Wonderful Wadricka, Caring Carol, Joyful JoAnn, Mysterious Matthew, Luminous Lewis and Teachable Terrence. *"It is finished."*

"If you eat well, you must speak well." As such, thanks to my former students, colleagues and friends at Cuyahoga Community College, Cleveland, Ohio, for fostering an environment conducive for my stabilization and growth. My heartfelt thanks to Professor Marla J. Colvin who piqued my curiosity and provoked me to re-examine, dissect and digest, embrace and embody ancient ideas in a fresh, new light. Thank you. Thank you, thank you all for teaching me so much.

Thanks to my mentor, Dr. Dorothy Vick Smith, whose intelligence and beauty is soothingly satiating and phenomenally catalytic. Your unwavering willingness to share of yourself is meaningful. I'm certain that I'd like to be like you when I've grown.

Gratitude to my honorable guides whose sum and substance has been immeasurably instructive on my journey. *"... And a child shall lead them:"* Matthew Stepanek, Rev. Dr. Theo and Jan Triplett, Dr. Martin Luther King, Langston Hughes, Iyanla Vanzant, J. California Cooper, Paul Laurence Dunbar, Charles Fillmore, Joel Goldsmith, Stephen V. Covey, James Baldwin, Oprah Winfrey, The Foundation for Inner Peace, James Weldon Johnson, Don Miguel Ruiz, Cornell West,

Khalil Gibran, Zora Neal Hurston, Maya Angelou, Malcolm X, Gary Zukav, Howard Thurman, Ralph Ellison, Dr. Stephen Hawking, Dr. Peter Gomes, Richard Wright, Ernest Holmes, Toni Morrison, Sam Cooke, Rev. James Cleveland, Shirley Caesar, Marchette Chute, and Alice Walker, just to name a few.

Also, thanks to my former English instructor, Mrs. Georgia A. Lewis, the master artist, whose pregnant words will eternally remain etched in the womb of my mind. Finally, may love, respect, and abundant blessings continue to be showered upon Ms. Aretha Franklin, who, I think is, indisputably so, the Queen of Soul. *And so it is!* Thank you for reminding me.

"But many who are first will be last, and the last first." First, and foremost, THANK YOU GOD, in whom I live, move, and have my being.

<u>Dedication</u>

This book is dedicated to my dear mother, Channie Mae Abby, who

prayed for me

Carolyn Henderson-McNeal, a Mississippi black pearl

and

In remembrance of George Gregory Boykin

August 10, 2002

They softly went, but sure, and at the End

Found that the Lord of Pilgrims was their Friend

When thou hast told the World of all these things

Then turn about, my Book, and touch these strings;

Which, if but touched, will such musick make,

They'll make a Cripple dance, a Giant quake.

Those Riddles that lie couch'd within thy breast,

Freely propound, expound: And for the rest

Of thy mysterious lines, let them remain

For those who nimble Fancies shall them gain.

Now may this little Book a blessing be

To those that love this little Book, and me:

And may its Buyer have no cause to say,

His money is but lost, or thrown away;

Yea, may this Second Pilgrim yield that Fruit

As may with each good Pilgrim's fancy suit;

And may it persuade some that go astray,

To turn their Foot and Heart to the right Way

John Bunyan
THE PILGRIM'S PROGRESS

TABLE OF CONTENTS

Then the voice which I heard from heaven spoke to me again and

said, "Go, take the little book which is open in the hand of the angel

who stands on the sea and on the earth." And I went to the angel and

said to him, "Give me the little book." And he said to me, "Take and

eat it; and it will make your stomach bitter, but it will be as sweet as

honey in your mouth." And I took the little book out of the angel's

hand and ate it, and it was as sweet as honey in my mouth. But when I

had eaten it, my stomach became bitter. And he said to me, "You

must prophesy again about many peoples, nations, tongues, and

kings."

Revelation 10:8-11

The Holy Bible

New King James Version

PREFACE

In the simple yet profoundly poignant words of Ernest Holmes:
"Change Your Thinking. Change Your Life." Before the beginning of
time, woman was created and placed at the pinnacle, the apex of
creation. She was endowed with inalienable rights, divine traits and
attributes of a majestic Creator desirous of mirroring herself in
manifestation. Further, she was given the internal, external, and
eternal capacity of power and dominion to rule the world royally.

What happened?

Unfortunately, the trials of life have left the majority of us
disappointed, disillusioned and completely dismissive of our true
heritage and identity. Like prodigals, individually and collectively, we
have been meandering down various pathways and crossroads in
search of the answer and meaning of life's little riddle. More often
than not, these efforts have proven frustrating and futile, thus leading
to bitterness and resentment compounded. How do we solve this
maxim called life and find solace and success in a world seemingly so

antagonistic toward our good? How do we find our way out of a vicious maze of disgust and disenchantment and take claim of our pot of gold at the end of life's rainbow?

Well, I am convinced that *remembrance* is the key to solving the so-called mystery of life. Therefore, let's get it back like it was before it got like it is! *".... And she heard the voice of the Lord God walking in the garden in the cool of the day..."* Remember our former relationship with God. *"...And she came to herself..."* Remember who God is. *"I AM that I AM."* Remember who God said you are. *"This is my beloved Daughter in whom I am well pleased."* Remember what God said you could do. *"For with God nothing shall be impossible."* And, finally, *remember* why God said you could do it. *"I and my Father are one."* Remembrance. Remembrance. Remembrance.

The book cover, designed by artist and friend, Jean Bean, undeniably speaks volumes. Underneath the dross of what you think you know, who you think you are, and what you think you see and feel is your true God self longing to be revealed, acknowledged, and accepted.

"Who told you that you were naked?"

Each of us, individually, alone, must unravel the riddle and reclaim our own inherent possession and fulfill our own destiny. We must delve within the deep recesses of our souls because the answer to life's problem lies hidden in the heart of our minds.

"Arise and shine for thy light has come and the glory of the Lord has risen upon thee!" Therefore, let us not resist, but let us *recall*, and let the journey begin again.

A GRACIOUS INVITATION

John 5:6

Isaiah 1:18

John 1:39,43

The door to the Church is now wide open.

1

Christina Abby

<u>MAMA PRAYED FOR ME</u>

Genesis 18:14; Jeremiah 33:3

My loving mother, she prayed for me

The best thing she could do

Philippians 4:6; 2 Thessalonians 5:17

She said, "Baby, I care"

But, more importantly, God loves you

Romans 8:38,39; 1John 4:8

She came to the Pacific Northwest

When my spirit and body was broken down

Luke 10:33-37; 1 Corinthians 10:24

She faithfully visited and brought me goodies

When I saw no one else around

Mark 12:43,44

She rode the bus from Mississippi

To help to see me through

Philippians 2:3-5; 1 Corinthians 12:25,26

She prayed, cooked and cleaned

Always asking "What more can I do?"

Acts 9:6; Psalms 18:3

She bowed down on her humble knees

Tears rolling down her face

James 4:6,8,10; John 11:33,35

I wasn't sure what she'd do next

She sang Amazing Grace

James 5:13; Luke 18:7,8

She said she saw a blinding light

Shining in on her instead

Isaiah 60:1; 1 Peter 1:12,13

A choir began to sing that song

There's A Brighter Day Ahead

John 16:20,21; Psalms 30:5

She informed me of prayer warrior

Just grieving and praying for me

Hebrews 12:1,2; Proverbs 11:10

That look of God in her eyes

Behold, if you could see!

Ezekiel 1:26-28; Revelation 19:12

She said "Chris, Stop your crying, Baby"

Christian is definitely at rest

Mark 5:39; 1 Thessalonians 4:13-16

No matter what you're feeling now

My God always knows what's best!

John 11:4; Romans 8:18

My soul is really satisfied now

No chains, no burdens, I'm free!

Isaiah 10:27; Psalms 107:9

I thank God, and I love my Mama

Lord knows she prayed for me

Matthew 26:13; John 3:33

A mother's love has healing properties.

UNRAVELIN' THE RIDDLE

Mark 4:34

You can appear shallow and be, oh, so deep

John 7:24; 1 Corinthians 2:10,14

You can possess nothing and still have a heap

Luke 12:15; Luke 15:31

You can be by yourself and not be alone

Hebrews 13:5; Matthew 28:20

You can reach adulthood and not be grown

Matthew 3:17; Luke 18:17; Isaiah 11:6

You can be in and still be out

John 18:36; John 17:14-16

7

You can be all-powerful and have no clout

Psalms 37:35,36; 1 Corinthians 3:19,20

You can be torn apart and yet be sealed

2 Corinthians 1:21,22; Ephesians 1:13,14

You can be tossed to and fro and be standing still

Romans 7:15,24; 2 Chronicles 20:15,17

You can be sane but outta your mind

Isaiah 45:7; John 19:10,11

You can have 20/20 and be totally blind

Luke 8:10; Isaiah 43:8

You can be old and still be young

Psalms 92:12-14; John 8:58

You can speak the truth and not use your tongue

Luke 21:13-15; Proverbs 17:27,28

You can be in a puddle and still be clean

John 1:29; Luke 5:13

You can be ready ripe and yet be green

John 10:30; John19:30

You can sway far left or far right and still be in the middle

Psalms 139:7,8; Romans 8:38,39

But if you ain't got the concept, you won't get the riddle

Colossians 1:26,27; Luke 24:45

Sacred secrets He'll unfold. The mysteries of God can only be revealed to, by, and through the word of God.

<u>FEEDING THE FLOCK</u>

Psalms 37:3

Chile, we went grazin' ovah yon'r in de pasture today and Shepherd

brought us som' real good soul food. You shole did miss a good meal

Chile. "Well, what did y'all have?" Chile, you missed it. "Well, ain't

you evah gon' tell me?!" Hold yer horses, I'm gittin' to it. You jus'

don't know what you miss'd Chile.

Matthew 4:4

Chile, we wuz in sheep heav'n and we grazed til we got full. And

Chile we…."Go 'head, tell me, pleez." Anyway, for our main course,

we ate off Luke's plate. And it wuz so good cuz der's a variety of

stuff. You know you and me both lak dat variety cuz it makes our

stomachs feel kinda good. I do lak dat Luke, but my fav'rite is dat

John! Come to thank 'bout it, I kinda lak dat Isaiah, Jeremiah, and

Ezekiel too. Not to mention dem Psalms and dem Proverbs. Chile,

dem deh Proverbs dey shole…."Well, ain't you evah gon' finish?!"

"Jus' talk and sey it!"

John 10:5,27

Lak I wuz seyin,' dem deh Proverbs is jus' full of mutha wit. "Go

'head, git to de point!" Well, anyway, He tole us dis heh story 'bout

dis heh King dat invit'd som' rich peoples to de big house. Dey sey

dey wuz gon' come but when de King sent His slaves to *remind* 'em,

e'vahbody wuz busy. You know, dey had dem flim, flam 'xcuses. Jus'

lak when…."Den what happn'?"

Luke 14:16-20

11

Well, dis heh King wuz disappoint'd cuz He had all dis food and stuff cook'd up for 'em. So He tole His slaves to go out in de streets and git evahbody dat dey could so dey could fill up de big house. Nat'ually, der wuz a lotta hun'ry folk out der dat came in heh to enjoy a free meal. You know how we do. Jus' lak dat time when dat ole wolf come ovah c'here and wuz spongin' off us! And you know 'bout dat oth'r time when dem snakes wuz.…..."And what did de King sey?"

"Spit it out!"

Luke 21:19; Hebrews 4:12

Chile, don't git so touchy, touchy, touchy! Anyway, dat King seys dat dem ones dat didn't come wuzn't gon' git no mo' invites. "Dey miss'd out, huh?" Yep, jus' lak dem two legg'd folk sey, dey gon' be a day late and dollar short! "I'm gittin' full wit you jus' talkin' 'bout it." "I shole hate I miss'd it!" And dat ain't all Chile. "Well, what, what, what else happn'd?"

12

Luke 14:21-24

Den Shepherd led us back ovah yon'r and gave us sumthin' to drank

from Jeremiah's cup. I can't *remembrance* what it wuz cuz I wuz too

full 'bout den. You know when I git too full my *remembrance* b'gin

to fail me. I don't know why, but dat's always ben de case, e'en when

I…..“Go 'head, go 'head, talk and sey it!!!”

Psalms 23:5; John 7:38; Psalms 34:8

Anyway fuh sho' what'en'evah it wuz, it felt jus' lak fire! “Sho'

nuff!” Yeaaah Chile and I wuzn't de only one dat felt lak dat either.

E'en Shepherd wuz grinnin' 'bout it! Chile, we commenc'd ta runnin'

and shoutin' 'round dat pasture jus' to cool off! Ooooh Chile, you

shole did miss som' good somt'eat. “I b'lieve I did!” “Den what

happn'd?”

13

Jeremiah 20:9; Acts 5:39; Hebrews 4:12

Fin'lly, Shepherd open'd dem gates so dat dem stray or dem lost sheep could join our flock. When He did dat, 'bout five, six, or sev'n of 'em come ovah ch'ere. Der goes one right der. Let me go ovah heh and talk wit 'em. "Ain't you evah gon' finish first?" Ooh yeah, I can't *remembrance* how many of 'em it wuz dat come ovah ch'ere cuz you know dat when I gits too full my *remembrance* b'gin to...."You said dat already!" "What, what else happn'd?!"

Revelation 3:20; John 1:39,43

You know Shepherd is so nice. He den tole dem new lambs dat He would giv' 'em a grazin' buddy to help 'em feel mo' comfortable in our pasture. Der goes mine right der. Let me go ovah heh and help a sistah out. Anyway, Honey Chile, dat shole wuz som' good eatin.'

You shole did miss sumptin' good! "I b'lieve I did! Makes me wanna

stomp!"

John 14:26; Psalms 42:1,2

The Lord is the Shepherd and truth is truth irregardless of the

language spoken.

Christina Abby

JOHN'S REVELATION

Revelation 21:1-5

I, John, was driving along this picturesque stretch of the countryside

Just enjoying my cruise and the beauty of the day

Psalms 91:1

I was overwhelmed by the glory I was seeing

I wasn't paying attention; I mistakenly turned the wrong way

Proverbs 1:33; John 15:4

I went barreling down a one-way street

Just me at first, oh what a relief

Luke 15:12,13

Nothing or no one could have ever prepared me

For the next moment, seemingly lifetime, of sorrow and grief

Genesis 3:17-19

In a twinkling of an eye, my life changed

I caused a horrible, horrible accident

Genesis 2:17; 1 Corinthians 15:51-53

I killed the hopes and dreams of two people

And out of my car window I went

John 3:19

I severed my spinal column

What happened to the other people I really didn't care

2 Chronicles 7:14

They've got the best of the two evils

Hecky, I'm now in a wheelchair

John 11:4

I've gotta go to rehab

I really don't wanna try

John 5:6,7

I wish they would just leave me alone

God, I wish I could just disappear or die

Psalms 22:1; 1 Kings 19:4

They're wasting their money and my time

It won't do me no doggone good

Matthew 8:13

I'm a paraplegic

I thought that was well understood

Ezekiel 37:3-14; John 12:16

That physical therapist Jan

She always getting on my case

Luke 4:43; Acts 13:47

"John, you can do it," she says

You can recover and leave "that" place

Luke 4:18,19; Psalms 103:11-14

I'm gonna get on her nerves one of these days

At least, my mission is to try

Ezra 4:4,5; Luke 23:34; Romans 11:25

Yet, she just keep pushing and encouraging me

What I'm selling, she just won't buy

Proverbs 23:23; James 2:19

I'm sick of all these happy go lucky people

My doctor, my therapist, and the counselor assigned to me

Proverbs 11:14; Acts 18:9,10; John 10:3,4,27

Their unsolicited advice ain't really welcomed

Why don't they just go ahead, leave me alone, and let me be!

Revelation 3:20

I went to see that Jan again today

I really vented, told her some pretty horrible stuff

James 3:6; Proverbs 18:21

Out of anger and frustration with me

She told me "Enough is Enough!"

John 19:30

She referred me to my counselor

I had to visit her, per her request

Psalms 119:91; Luke 1:68,69

I was looking forward to seeing her again

Huh, I had to get some things off my chest!

Matthew 11:28-30; Mark 6:31

She told me that she liked as a person

In fact, I think you're a very nice dude

Romans 2:11; Romans 11:18; Acts 10:34

But one thing I hafta tell you

You've got a funky attitude

Psalms 78:9-11

You have a putrid aroma

And you sure do stink

2 Corinthians 2:16; 1 Corinthians 15:36; 2 Corinthians 4:16-18

This world doesn't owe you anything

"Now, what do you think?"

Isaiah 55:8; Proverbs 16:3

Completely surprised

My mouth almost hit the floor

Hebrew 4:12

I did what comes naturally

I took a b-line for the door

Romans 10:21; Hebrews 3:15

I told her she was insensitive

I'm a paraplegic, "Can't you see?!"

1 John 1:5; John 1:5

I'm in a wheelchair

You should have pity on me

John 10:34,35

She paused for a second

Pity, I'm sorry, I haven't any

Acts 3:4-6

But compassion and honesty

Now, that I have a plenty!

Luke 10:33-37; Hosea 6:6; Lamentations 3:22

I rolled right on out the door

Admittedly, I was mad as hell

John 3:19; James 3:16

Whoever would listen to me

That's exactly the person I was gone tell!

John 12:43; Psalms 118:8

There ain't no lie in the truth. It truly can set us free. John just can't accept. He will.
Let's move forward and see.

John 1:39,43

I avoided her like the plague

You knew that I would

Matthew 23:37,38; Isaiah 45:8,9

She said couldn't really help me

And I didn't think that she could

John 3:19; Matthew 8:13

I spoke with my doctor about it

My family had already given up on me

Psalms 68:6

He told me that he couldn't help me either

The Counselor is who I really needed to see

Isaiah 9:6; Isaiah 45:22

He said, "Please, please go back to see her"

She really has your best interest at heart

Isaiah 1:18; 2 Chronicles 7:14

We all want to help you move forward

But, first, you've got to do your part

Mark 1:15; 1 John 1:9

I had a chance to do some intent soul-searching

And lo and behold, in came a bold, bright light

Isaiah 60:1; Revelation 22:16

As much as I really hated it

I knew, I knew they all had been right

Luke 24:45; John 8:32

*Finally, John is on the road to recovery. He's tapped that bright light
inside you and me. He's about to overcome his challenges. Again,
let's move forward and see.*

25

1 John 5:4,5; John 16:33

I went back to see her

To everybody, I truly needed to make amends

1 Corinthians 14:40; Matthew 5:23,24

I told her she wasn't responsible

For the spiritual condition I was in

Romans 8:5-8; John 4:23,24

She smiled and said, "I'm proud of you"

"I had faith, John." "I knew that you could"

Mark 11:22,23; Hebrews 11:1,6,29

It was all a question of when, John

I didn't know when, John, when you would

Galatians 6:9; 2 Thessalonians 2:6; John 10:16

Jan was right

I have left "that" place

Isaiah 48:10; Proverbs 25:4

Determined and empowered

I'm now in the race

Luke 24:49; Acts 1:8; John 20:22

Foolishly locked in my own prison

In manacles of misery and despair

Psalms 69:5; Psalms 73:22

Like an old, idled car

I was getting nowhere

1 Kings 18:21; Psalms 119:59

I've changed my funky attitude

27

It's made a big difference, you see

Zechariah 4:6; 1 Corinthians 15:51

Yes, I'm a paraplegic

But that won't stop me!

John 4:29; John 9:25

A little advice to my audience

Trust me, I know where you've been

Psalms 119:67,71

Healing and empowerment is truly easy

It comes from within

Luke 17:20,21; Romans 2:28,29

Just change your attitude and persevere

It's amazing what the two can do

Psalms 119:59; Romans 5:3-5; 2 Corinthians 4:7-10

Like neosporin and penicillin

Effective: They're tried and true!

Psalms 12:6; Acts 5:32; John 3:33

Such is the story of John

How does it end?

Revelation 22:1-6

Well, if you ain't in the race

You shole can't win!

Ecclesiastes 9:11; 1 Corinthians 9:24-27

A conscious relationship is the only requirement.

<u>WOE AND WISDOM</u>

Psalms 39:10-13

Knock, Knock, Father

Oh wretched me

Romans 7:24; Ezekiel 37:1-7

I once was blind

But now I see

Isaiah 60:1; Revelation 3:19

Heal my soul, Lord

I was ignorant of You

Psalms 41:4; Acts 3:17

I repent wholeheartedly

That's all I know to do

Mark 1:15; 1 Samuel 13:14

What I did Lord

I now know wasn't right

John 12:16; Luke 24:45

Restore my joy

Please hear me tonight

Psalms 51:12; Psalms 99:8

Revive me, dear Lord

I've learnt my mistake

Psalms 143:11; Psalms 119:59

Purge me with hyssop

How long will it take?

Psalms 51:7; Psalms 79:5; Hebrews 12:11

Don't take your Holy Spirit

What then would I do?

John 6:63; Acts 17:28

I'm gone keep on knocking, Lord

Because I'm through without You!

Genesis 32:24-26; Psalms 119:67,71

When knowledge truly, honestly comes, wisdom purely, surely lingers.

Christina Abby

upside down

Psalms 147:5; Psalms 92:5

What happens to a dream deferred?

Does it dry up
Like a raisin in the sun
Or fester like a sore –
And then run?
Does it stink like rotten meat?
Or crust and sugar over –
Like a syrupy sweet?
Maybe it just sags
like a heavy load

Or does it explode?

"Poetry is the human soul entire, squeezed like a lemon or a lime,
drop by drop, into atomic words."

Langston Hughes

What you call doing, I call done

John 1:29; Luke 4:21

It is finished!

34

What you call many, I call One

Deuteronomy 6:4; Ephesians 4:4-6

Oneness with the Source is oneness with all manifestation.

What you call the what, I call the why?

Genesis 3:11,12; Jeremiah 18:15,16

Within the problem lies its own solution.

What you call an apple, I call a pie

Revelation 21:1-4

Begin with the end in mind.

What you call ending, I call beginning

2 Corinthians 5:17

Behold! I do a new thing!

What you call losing, I call winning

2 Chronicles 20:17; Romans 8:31

The battle is waged in the mind.

What you call giving, I call receiving

Luke 6:38; Exodus 35:5; 2 Corinthians 1:21,22

No investment, no return. No deposit; no withdrawal.

What you call living, I call believing

Genesis 1:26,27

I believe I'll make me a world!

What you call high, I call low

Isaiah 14:11-15; John 13:16; John 3:30

Father, glorify Thy name!

What you call deep, I call shallow

1Corinthians 3:19,20; 2 Corinthians 3:3; Colossians 2:8

Philosophy is great food for thought that can enlighten the mind. However, it has proven ineffectual in transforming the heart- the temple of God's familiar.

What you call low, I call high

James 4:10; Proverbs 15:33

Validation is indeed veneration.

What you call the mind, I call the eye

Luke 11:34-36; Mark 8:18

In the mind's eye is the answer to the who, the what, the when, the how, the where, and the why.

What you call transitory, I call static

Malachi 3:6; Luke 6:47,48; Psalms 11:3

God is the rock that will never roll!

What you call the basement, I call the attic

Genesis 1:31; Psalms 82:6,7

Christina Abby

Remembrance is the rhyme and reason of life's little riddle.

What you call secular, I call divine

Genesis 1:2; Psalms 104:30

Inspiration is the Mother/Father of invention.

What you call now, I call "in the meantime"

Jeremiah 29:11-14; John 10:16

Thy kingdom come. Thy will be done!

What you call evil, I call good

Genesis 1:31; 1 Timothy 1:8; James 1:17

There's a God-sent message in every murky little moronic mess. Its all good because its all God.

What you call mystical, I call misunderstood

John 1:5; John 12:16

I am God's co-pilot.

What you call a curse, I call a blessing

Psalms 139:12; Genesis 50:20

Life teaches us wonderful lessons if we would but STOP! THINK! LOOK! LISTEN!

What you call conforming, I call digressing

Romans 12:2; Isaiah 29:16; Romans 8:6-8

We are spiritual beings going through a human experience, not human beings going through a spiritual experience.

What you call the cause, I call the effect

Genesis 1:3

Which came first, the chicken or the egg?

What you call attentiveness, I call neglect

Matthew 23:23-25; Luke 11:39,40

Man is morally impotent and needs the grace of God to stand erect.

What you call the effect, I call the cause

Christina Abby

John 1:3; Psalms 100:3; Exodus 3:5

I AM because God IS.

What call a boo, I call an applause

Isaiah 2:22; John 12:43

Only the ego needs massaging. The Spirit just is!

What you call comfort, I call need

Luke 12:18,19

Comfort and serenity lies in the Creator, not the creature nor his/her creations.

What you call benevolence, I call greed

Matthew 6:3,4; Mark 11:17

When you do what you do without expectation, you'll never be disappointed.

When you say far, I say near

Proverbs 18:24; Ephesians 2:13

God IS wherever I AM.

What you call procrastination, I call fear

Romans 8:15; 2 Timothy 1:7

Why are you so fearful?

What you call in, I call out

Matthew 5:16; Matthew 6:22,23

The mirror reflects inwardly outwardly.

What you call disenfranchisement, I call clout

John 15:20; Psalms 118:22,23

The Lord has need of her.

When you say out, I say in

Luke 17:20,21; 1 John 4:4

Be internally motivated instead of externally driven.

What you call ignorance, I call the universal sin

Acts 3:17; 1 Peter 1:14

Ignorance, apathy, and fear are a deadly mix. Father, forgive us for we know not what we do.

What you call division, I call multiplication

Isaiah 6:8; Acts 20:35; Hebrews 6:14

What you call giving, I call receiving.

What you call satisfaction, I call starvation

John 4:32; John 9: 39-41

He who thinks he knows everything knows nothing; yet, what he ought to know is that nobody can ever know everything except God!

What you call subtraction, I call addition

Proverbs 25:4; 1 Corinthians 15:36

i die daily.

What you call conversion, I call recognition

Luke 15:17,18; John 9:25

Arise and shine for thy light has come and the glory of the Lord has risen upon thee!

When you say up, I say down

Luke 11:2

As above, so below.

What you call the cross, I call the crown

Luke 24:26; John 7:24

The Philosopher's Stone lies far beneath the surface. Reality always rules and will always elude literalism.

When you say down, I say up

John 8:23,24; Ephesians 4:23; John 12:32

An open mind has a room with a view.

What you call a plate, I call a cup

John 7:38; John 16:20,21

My cup runneth over!

When you say lost, I say found

Luke 8:45, 46; Psalms 89:20

When you get serious about God, God's bound to get serious about you.

What you call square, I call round

Galatians 6:7

Bad choices will always produce bad results.

When you say loose, I say bound

John 8:33; Luke 9:49,50

A closed head, heart, and hand can neither give nor receive.

What you call silence, I call sound

1 Kings 19:11,12; Isaiah 30:15

Speak Lord for thy servant hears.

What you call loss, I call gain

Proverbs 25:4; Philippians 3:7,8; Luke 17:33

Repentance ensures redemption. Redemption promotes refinement. Refinement promises restoration. Restoration guarantees reciprocity.

What you call sunshine, I call rain

Psalms 78:23-25; James 5:18; 1 Kings 18:42-46

Like the protective nature of an umbrella, the Sun is shining even when it's raining.

What you call gain, I call loss

Mark 14:36; Matthew16:25,26

Only the ego can ease God out.

Whom you designate servant, I recognize as the boss

Mark 10:42,43; Luke 22:27

Heavenly help comes via human hearts and human hands.

What you call simple, I call profound

Proverbs 23:7

Methinks you are divine.

What you call a pinch, I call a pound

Luke 13:18-21; Galatians 5:9

Quantity doesn't necessarily reflect quality; free ain't always what its cooked up to be.

What you call profound, I call simple

John 1:1-3

Pantheism. Gnosticism. God is all there is and has no superior. Period!

What you call a frown, I call a dimple

Psalms 37:13; Psalms 2:4; Psalms 146:8,9

Its a comedy that life is a tragedy. Now if you really wanna hear and see God laugh, lay out your own 'damned' plans.

What you call empty, I call full

John 1:14; John 15:11

I and my Father are one.

When you say push, I say pull

Acts 9:3-6; 2 Corinthians 10:4,5

Canst thou hinder or retard the heart or hand of God?

What you call full, I call empty

Romans 10:2,3; 2 Corinthians 10:12; Luke 16:15

Before honor, there is humility.

What you call the gloom, I call the glee!

John 16:22; Galatians 5:22,23; Luke 10:41,42

This joy I've got, this world didn't give it to me and this world can't take it away!

What you call profane, I call sacred

Psalms 2:7,8; Matthew 3:17

The place where you stand is holy ground.

What you call the ego, I call the id

Matthew 19:6; Mark 10:9

United we stand. God bless the world.

What you call sacred, I call profane

Mark 7:6-9

Talk is cheap. I'd rather see a sermon than hear one any day.

What you call extreme fundamentalism, I call preposterously insane

Matthew 23:1-7; Hosea 6:6

Crazy is what crazy does!

What you call wrong, I call right

1 Corinthians 4:7; Romans 11:18; Matthew 7:1

Entry into heaven is not on a group-rate basis. God desires intimately personal relationships. Each one of us, individually, alone, must unravel our own riddle of life.

When you say daylight, I say midnight

Luke 11:5-10; Luke 18:7,8; Acts 16:25-34

The darkest hour always precedes the dawn.

What you call right, I call wrong

James 4:16; Psalms 75:7; Luke 18:9-14

Remember, God alone sets the standard.

What you call a dirge, I call a hallelujah song!

John 11:32-44; 2 Kings 4:19-37; 1 Samuel 1:5-20

From hurt to hallelujah! My soul is a witness.

What you call old, I call new

Psalms 92:12-14; Revelation 21:1; Luke 5:36-39

Great is Thy faithfulness. It is new every morning.

When you say yellow, I say blue

1 Kings 19:4; John 16:33

Every tub has got to sit on its own bottom!

What you call new, I call old

Psalms 93:1,2; Deuteronomy 32:7; John 8:58

All is vanity. The problem and its attending solution have been clearly, succinctly outlined in an old ancient Book.

When you say meekness, I say bold

Acts 4:31; John 19:11; Proverbs 28:1; Hebrews 4:16

True to our God; true to our native land.

What you call hatred, I call love

Romans 13:10; 1 Corinthians 13:1-13

Love cultivates and motivates and does not dominate or eradicate.

When you say below, I say above

Luke 11:2; Colossians 3:2

And so it is!

What you call the ebb, I call the flow

Mark 4:26,27; John 21:18; John 3:8

The whole world is a stage and everyone plays his or her part.

When you say above, I say below also

Psalms 27:13; 2 Corinthians 4:3,4

Heaven and earth are states of consciousness.

What you call a woman, I call a man

Genesis 2:21-23; Galatians 3:28

God is Spirit.

What you call the foot, I call the hand

Luke 6:8-10; Psalms 37:23,24; Jeremiah 10:23; Psalms 78:72

The hand of God animates the feet of men.

When you say filthy, I say clean

Luke 5:13; John 15:3

Think and act as though you are and you will be.

What you call barren, I call green

Genesis 3:11,12; Psalms 68:6; John 3:19

It's mine own fault!

What you call hot, I call cold

Revelation 3:17; 2 Peter 2:17

When you know better, you'll do better.

When you say bought, I say sold

Luke 21:3,4; Proverbs 23:23

A souled out soul can never be bought.

What you call cold, I call hot

Mark 5:30,31; John 11:40

Blessed are the pure in heart for they shall taste, see, hear, feel and know God.

What you think is, I think and know not

Isaiah 55:8; 1 Corinthians 13:12

Beneath the veneer of the illusion lies the truth and the final conclusion.

What you call first, I call last

John 6:27; Matthew 6:19,20

They've got the vapors!

53

What you call the future, I call the present and the past

Psalms 46:1; Luke 23:43

Carpe Diem!

What you call hunger, I call thirst

Psalms 42:1,2; Psalms 143:5,6

Wise men still seek Him.

When you say last, I say first

Matthew 6:33; Luke 12:31,32

Put first things first.

When you say more, I say less

Proverbs 17:27,28; Proverbs 29:11

He who is the most dogmatic is the least pragmatic. We should listen as twice as much as we talk. That's why God gave us two ears and one mouth.

What you call failure, I call success

Acts 13:30; John 11:40

Success is just failure turned upside down. A setback is actually a launching pad for a comeback.

What you think is less, I know to be more

Act 3:2-6

The eyes are the windows to the soul.

Whom you despise, I truly adore

1 Corinthians 4:7; Luke 10:33

One man's trash is another man's treasure. One man's poison is another man's candy.

What you call teaching, I call learning

1 Corinthians 3:6; Luke 4:36

The more you sow, the more you'll see and know. The sower sows the word.

What you call spending, I call earning

Psalms 1:1-3; Joshua 1:8

If you don't sow, you certainly won't grow.

When you say peace, I say confusion

Jeremiah 8:11; 1 Thessalonians 5:3

Uncertainty and inconsistency in purpose produces confusion worst confounded.

What you call your reality, I call 'just an illusion'

Mark 4:35; Isaiah 29:16; John 18:36

Flipping the script makes the journey a pleasantly wonderful trip!

What you call fragmented, I call whole

Jeremiah 8:22; Psalms 138:8

Trade in your pieces and God will give you His peace.

What you call the mind, I call the soul

Genesis 2:7; Mark 8:36

E=mc2. It is well. It is well. It is well with my soul.

What you call whole, I call part

1 Corinthians 2:9; Ephesians 3:20

Words fail me. Unimaginable. Unknowable. Unexplainable.

What you call the ear, I call the heart

Luke 24:32

Give them something that they can feel.

When you say seek, I say find

Luke 15:17; Hebrews 8:8-12

Remembrance. Remembrance. Remembrance.

What you call the eye, I call the mind

Luke 24:45; Mark 7:34

A ready, ripe, and receptive mind is but destined to blossom.

When you say meat, I say bread

John 6:33; 1 Corinthians 10:17

Trust, dwell, and feed on His faithfulness.

What you call the heart, I call the head

Psalms 4:4; Psalms 19:14

How can you meditate with your heart unless the consciousness of the act resides in your head?

What you call darkness, I call light

Genesis 1:3; Psalms 30:5

I'm so glad trouble don't last always.

When you say weakness, I say might

Luke 1:37; Luke 18:27; 2 Corinthians 12:9

One with God is a majority.

What you call dumb, I call bright

John 1:4; 2 Peter 2:16

Think and see with your own mind. Be careful in allowing others self-serving, warped perception(s) of who you are define and determine who you might be, who you can be, and who you will be.

What you call the depth, I call the height

1 Corinthians 15:42-46; Psalms 85:11

Still I rise. I Rise! I Rise! I Rise!

What you call temporary, I call permanent

Hebrews 1:10-12; Psalms 119:89

Que Sera Sera? Whatever will be will be.

When you say straight, I say bent

John 7:18; Proverbs 27:2; Luke 3:4-6

Christina Abby

Pride expressed internally is called wisdom. Pride expressed externally is known as folly.

What you call permanent, I call temporary

Luke 4:5-7; Proverbs 25:19; Psalms 118:8

Man is fickle and will disappoint, disillusion, then dismiss you.

What you call double-mindedness, I call the perpetual adversary

James 2:19; Isaiah 45:22; Isaiah 26:3

My mind is playing tricks on me.

What you call tragedy, I call triumph

Acts 13:30; 1 Corinthians 15:55

God always has a ram in the bush!

What you call an abyss, I call a bump

Proverbs 24:16; Psalms 37:24

Never underestimate the resiliency of an indomitable divine-human spirit.

60

What you call triumph, I call tragedy

1 Kings 21:1-16; Proverbs 16:4

All closed eyes ain't sleep and all goodbyes ain't gone.

What I call providence, You call serendipity

1 Corinthians 13:11; John 4:6-29

I once was blind, but now I see; was lost, but now I'm found.

What you call dead, I call alive

Luke 24:5; John 11:25; Luke 20:38

If God is Life and Life is God, doesn't it seem a bit contradictory to think that God/Life can die?

What you call ritualism, I call shuck and jive

Luke 12:1; Luke 11:39,40

Religiosity breeds separation while spirituality fosters unification.

Christina Abby

When you say poor, I say rich

Psalms 2:7,8; Luke 15:31

Unclaimed possessions are easily stolen by the enemy.

What you call the glamour, I call the gilded glitch

James 1:11; 2 Corinthians 11:14

Pretty is what pretty does! All that glitters isn't really gold and all kinds of substance can't satisfy the soul.

What you think is a lie, I know to be true

1 John 2:21; Psalms 89:35; 2 Timothy 1:12

And you shall know the truth and the truth shall set you free.

When you say how, I say who?

Exodus 3:14

Know God. That's all that needs to be known.

What you call truth, I call the big fat lie

Genesis 3:4,5; John 8:44; 1 John 4:6

Let him who stole steal no more. That which I AM seeking, I already AM.

What you call unmitigated deceit, I call the modus operandi

John 10:10; 1 Peter 5:8; John 10:34,35

We've been had. We've been hoodwinked. We have been bamboozled!

When you say go, I say wait

Psalms 27:14; Isaiah 40:31; Psalms 104:27

Patience is a virtue.

What you call early, I call late

Proverbs 1:28; Psalms 27:8

The soul will remain restless, aimless, and barren until it find its way back home.

When you say wait, I say go

Christina Abby

2 Kings 7:3-6; Acts 18:9,10; John 2:5

Fear immobilizes even when your season has come. Remember, you'll never get anywhere fast if you choose to stay stuck on stupid and parked on dumb.

When you say it isn't, I say it tis so!

Acts 4:19,20; John 3:33

Let the redeemed of the Lord say so whom He has redeemed from the hand of the enemy.

What you call big, I call small

Luke 13:18-21; Luke 10:21; Isaiah 11:6.

Little is much when God is in it.

When you say short, I say tall

Luke 19:1-10; Mark 8:24,25

Acknowledge. Accept. Surrender. Then, miraculously the truth, already known, will graciously, gloriously be revealed.

What you call small, I call big

64

Luke 18:17; Mark 4:30-32

And the least shall be the greatest.

What you call your life, I call your gig

Acts 13:47; Luke 4:18,19; 1 Corinthians 6:20

A Charge To Keep, A God To Glorify.

When you say unjust, I say kind

Luke 15:12-13,31-32; Jeremiah 29:11-14

If God doesn't reside at your house, guess who moved?

What you call the fruit, I call the vine

John 15:1,5; Psalms 91:1

Reclaim and repossess the vine and you're guaranteed the fruit.

What you call pain, I call healing

John 11:4; Hebrews 12:10-12

Ironically, while pain hurts it simultaneously heals. I was reborn when I was broken.

What you think is hidden, I think and know to be revealing

Luke 12:2,3; Psalms 19:1,2

It ain't no secret what God can do. What He's done for others, He'll do the same for you.

When you say have, I say be

Acts 17:28; Luke 6:40

Truth is demonstration. To be or not to be, now that is the question?

What you assess costly, I attest to be free

1 Corinthians 2:12; Ephesians 2:8

Man's principal problem is his ignorance of his ignorance. Therefore, ignorance is at the heart and soul of all of life's struggles.

What you call bondage, I call liberty

2 Corinthians 3:16,17; Psalms 144:9,10; Psalms 45:1

Free your mind and your heart, body, and soul will sing.

Because what you call you, I call Me

Luke 13:16

Sometimes we all need to go backwards and give ourselves a check up from the neck up. STOP, THINK, and LOOK. Like a resplendent sunbeam that gloriously radiates the majestic splendor of the sun and like an infinitesimal wave that fuels, propels, and reverberates the massive presence of an ocean, One word, One idea can arrest the soul and literally revolutionize the mind.

Romans 11:33,34

Gods

The ivory gods,
And the ebony gods,
And the gods of diamond and jade
Sit silently on their temple shelves
While the people
Are afraid.
Yet the ivory gods,
And the ebony gods,
And the gods of diamond-jade,
Are only silly puppet gods
That the people themselves
Have made.

Langston Hughes

Depth defines dimension. Dimension determines destiny.

Christina Abby

<u>DARK WITNESSES</u>

Matthew 10:16; 1 John 4:1

Reverend Too Sharp

Armani suit, I do believe

Matthew 7:15,16

God said bow down and follow me

And a blessing is what y'all gone receive

Revelation 22:8,9; Psalms 118:8

God said He's gonna give it to y'all

Just have some faith in me

Mark 11:22; Proverbs 25:19

Blessings gonna come pouring down

Just keep on watching me and see!

Proverbs 14:15; John 1:39,43

Come on and praise God for what He's gonna do

Claim them blessings that I'm about to get for you!

Isaiah 17:10,11

Reverend Big Daddy

Yes, he's a preacher, Honey

John 7:24; Mark 12:38-40; Luke 11:39

God said dig a lil' deeper

Church, y'all gone hafta show me some mo' money!

Luke 12:15; 1 Timothy 6:10

Pastors ought not have to be broke and in no lurch

Matthew 21:13; Matthew 22:20,21

I'm telling y'all to put up or shut up

Else I'm gone hafta find me a new church!

Matthew 23:2-7; Mark 11:17

Reverend Smooth talker

Pastoral counseling is his forte, you see

Romans 16:17,18; Jude 16

He got too close for comfort wit Sistah Johnson

Lawd, I don't know what came over me!

Luke 6:45; Mark 7:18-23

God said we oughta forgive and forget

Cuz he ain't through with none of us yet!

Luke 6:40; Psalms 138:8

Y'all know I ain't lying and I'm telling the truth

70

If He came back tonight, what would some of y'all do?

John 8:44; 2 Corinthians 11:14,15

Some of y'all ain't gone be ready

And you know I'm right

Luke 6:41,42; 2 Corinthians 10:12

Y'all oughta start praying right now, saints

Lest He decides to come back tonight!

Mark 13:5,32

Moving right along. Sistah Johnson, play that song that I like so much. *"How I Got Ovah."* I may not be what I want to be, but I'm sure not what I used to be. God is so good! Can I get a witness?

Acts 5:32

Christina Abby

Stand up and clap your hands if you know what I'm talking about. I remembrance that Friday night like it was yesterday when I decided to preach the gospel. My soul looks back and wonder*!*

John 7:18; John 8:13

And God told me to ask you

How can you preach unless you've been sent?

Romans 10:14-16; Acts 13:9,10

He told me to say

Many are called, but some just went!

Job 1:6,7; Romans 8:30

Content without context is merely pretext.

<u>ON it's JOB</u>

Deuteronomy 6:4; Isaiah 45:7

Sowing discord

And watering confusion

1 Peter 5:8; 1 Corinthians 14:33

Fertilizing smokescreens

And creating illusions

1 Corinthians 13:12; Romans 12:2

Veiling the truth

And mesmerizing minds

2 Corinthians 4:3,4; 2 Corinthians 3:16

Accusing constantly

73

Cheating and lying

John 8:44; Acts 13:10

Instilling fear

And fueling distress

1 Kings 19:4; 2 Corinthians 4:8,9

Immobilizing intentions

And hampering progress

Luke 22:31,32; Ezra 4:4,5

Exploiting vulnerabilities

Encouraging disbelief

2 Corinthians 12:7-9; Luke 22:31,32

Provoking defiance

And fostering grief

Acts 5:2,3; Jonah 1:1-12

Violating boundaries

And instigating hate

2 Samuel 11:2-4; 1 Kings 21:5-16

Incarcerating souls

And stalling fate

Luke 11:2-4; John 10:16

Exalting itself

And acting all proud

Isaiah 14:12-15; Revelation 12:10,11; James 2:19

Transposing reality

And deceiving the crowd

Isaiah 26:3; Isaiah 45:22

Reconciliation of the seemingly opposites is the springboard to Christ-consciousness.

HOLD MY MULE

Luke 17:15-18

I ain't too proud, ashamed, nor do I apologize

For what'sen'evah you hear me say or do

Romans 1:16; Luke 9:26,27

I'm gone praise Him for all the thangs He's done for me

Now, I can't speak 'bout You, You, or You!

Psalms 34:1; Psalms 103:1,2

I libna cry, run, dance sing, grin, jump or laugh

Jus' don't you pay me no n'evahmind

2 Samuel 6:14,15; Psalms 45:1

Ask the folk that really, really know me

They'll tell ya, "she do that all the time!"

Isaiah 43:21; Acts 5:39

God has just been so good to me

And there ain't no question, taint no doubt

Romans 4:21; John 3:33

I just refuse to quench the Holy Spirit

So when I git happy, I'm shole gone shout!

Ephesians 4:30; 1 Thessalonians 5:19

Right now, I can feel His presence

It's evah so crystal clear, dear, and near

Acts 2:25-28; Proverbs 18:24

In fact, I'mma 'bout ta git happy right 'bout now

HOLD MY MULE, I thank I'll shout right ch'ere!

Luke 1:46-55; Jeremiah 15:15,16

Freedom of the soul is the wisdom of the eyes, heart, mind, and body.

COME SUNDAY

1 Peter 3:3,4

On Monday, she wuz Ms. Preen and Proper

She wouldn't e'en say hi

Galatians 6:3

On Tuesday, she wuz really Ms. Unapproachable

And I wuzn't gone e'en try

1 Corinthians 15:33; 2 Corinthians 6:17

On Wednesday, she wuz Ms. Jezebel, the Witch

God, she wuz controllin,' rude, and strewd

1 Kings 21:5-14

And Thursday wuzn't no bettah either

She wuz Mister and Missus Attitude!

Acts 5:2,3; Genesis 4:3-9

On Friday, she wuz Ms. Lillie, the Lioness

Just lurkin' and stalkin' her prey

Job 1:6,7; 1 Peter 5:8

And the world kept on turnin'

She wuz Ms. Queen Cobra on Sat-ur-day

Job 2:7

But ooooh, COME SUNDAY mornin'

Pretty in pank, and ooh jus' sooo sincere at heart

Romans 2:28,29

The most well rehearsed and seasoned actress on dat der stage

Lawd knows she sho' nuff played dat part!

Luke 11:39,40

Christina Abby

Hypocrites are people who are not themselves COME SUNDAY.

BE CAREFUL WHAT YOU PRAY FOR

Jeremiah 33:3

Why can't You answer my prayers sometimes

You know my flesh is weak

Mark 14:38; 2 Corinthians 12:9

Please, Lawd, hurry up and answer me

A blessing is what I seek

Mark 10:51

Lawd, I jus' want You to give me money

I'm askin' for such and such

Proverbs 4:7; James 4:3

I've got mo' than a lotta folk already

Lawd, I don't need dat much!

Luke 16:10-13; Mark 14:38

I met one of Your messengers, Lawd

He delivered Your word wit 'xtreme d'light

1 Chronicles 4:10

I truly wonder 'bout You Lawd

The way You came at me dat night!

Genesis 1:2

Lawd, stop revealin' all dis stuff to me

I jus' can't stand nor b'lieve all of dis

Luke 10:21-24; Deuteronomy 29:29

You've given me enough already, Lawd

Shucks, I'm already experiencin' heavenly bliss!

John 1:12,14; 1 Peter 2:9,10

Lawd, I jus' can't handle dis kinda unselfishness

Your grace is making my mind pretty hazy

2 Chronicles 1:10-12

Please slow down on dem gifts I've asked fuh

Lawd, You gon' drive me crazy!

Luke 6:38; Ephesians 3:20

Obedience is the floodgate and grace is an open-ended promissory note.

OLE FOLK WAYS

Psalms 19:7

Lawd, des misguided wise mens

Dey done gone all up in Your space

2 Timothy 3:7

Fumblin' out der in all Your glory

Why can't dey jus' stay in dey place?

Genesis 11:4-9

And Lawd, dey done built dem big ole thangs

I thank dey call 'em seven forty seven

Isaiah 2:22; Psalms 8:4

Don't dey know dat all God's chilluns got wangs

I'm gone git mine's when I gits to hea'ben

Isaiah 40:31; Luke 23:43

And Lawd, dey done heaped up all dem der riches

While others lak me, we go without

John 6:27; Luke 12:18,19

Dey ain't gon' take a cryin' dime wit 'em when dey leave dis heh place

Dey so smart, how come dey ain't figured dat one out?

Job 1:21; Psalms 49:10-12

And Lawd, dis clonin' mess got me kinda nervous

Who dey thank dey is, I jus' can't see?

Isaiah 45:7; Exodus 3:14

Hurry up and put a stop to dis heh nunsense Lawd

Cuz I don't want 'em cookin' up nuthin' dat's gon' be lookin' lak me!

Christina Abby

Psalms 118:8

And Lawd, You know I ain't got no learnin'

But dey ain't right, bright, smart, neither anyhow

2 Corinthians 11:6; 1 Corinthians 1:19-29

One thang I can put all my stock in, Lawd have mercy

Ev'ry knee is gon' bow!

Mark 15:2; Luke 14:11

Knowledge is the understanding that helps you make the peanut butter and bread. Wisdom is the instrument that helps you apply the spread.

THE RHYTHM OF LIFE

Mark 4:26-29

Something's going on

And I'm feeling the flow

John 3:8

The seemingly ultimate revelation

Can't define nor explain It cuz I really, really don't know

Romans 11:33,34

Consuming within

And exuding without

Proverbs 4:23; Luke 24:32

Poignant, yet elusive

Can't pinpoint nor quite figure It out

1 Kings 19:11,12; Psalms 139:6

A bubbling, burning passion

Pulsating my mind and veins

Hebrews 12:29; Jeremiah 20:9

Piercing my heart and soul

Quite impossible to contain

Hebrews 4:12; Job 38:31-36

Encouraging yet provoking

DO! GO NOW! MOVE!

John 19:30; John 5:8

Mystiquely mysterious

Inducing and controlling the groove

John 21:18; John 3:8

Expecting, respecting total surrender

Whispering, "Please, please, let it go"

Mark 14:36; Luke 23:46

Probing and disclosing

When you choose to just go with the flow

1 Corinthians 2:10-13

Life is a song worth singing. Choose, then listen and dance to its melodic beat.

Christina Abby

HE'S ALRIGHT

Acts 13:47

Girl, that's all you wanna talk about

Like them holy-rollies, why don't you go ahead and shout?

Act 4:19,20; Isaiah 43:21

That's alright, Girlfriend, shout I might

He saved my soul one glorious night

John 1:5

You really have changed Girl

Makes me not wanna come around

Ephesians 5:8; Acts 20:24

That's still alright Girlfriend

He healed my body when it was broken down

Isaiah 1:18; 2 Chronicles 7:14

Girl, I thought you wanted to teach

I can't tell now, all you do is preach

Luke 4:18,19

That's alright Girlfriend, you'd better listen to what I say

He coming back for all His saints one day

John 14:2-4; 1 Thessalonians 4:16,17

You need a vacation, Girl

Let's travel from coast to coast

1 Samuel 3:9; Romans 8:14

I've gotta stay put Girlfriend

Cuz I'm lead only by the Holy Ghost!

Proverbs 1:33; Psalms 32:8,9

Girl, you make me nervous

Talking that kinda talk

Acts 26:28,29; Zechariah 4:6

I'm so, so sorry Girlfriend

But in His straight pathway I must walk

Galatians 5:16; John 8:12

Girl, you're acting like a schoolgirl

That's just fell in love

Psalms 45:1; 1 Corinthians 13:1-13

That's alright Girlfriend

Have you ever seen an ascending dove?

John 1:32; Luke 24:11

Naw Girl! I'm just shocked and stunned

I just can't understand a word you say!

Luke 24:16; John 12:16

That's alright Girlfriend

All you gotta do is pray

Philippians 4:6; 1 Thessalonians 5:17

I've gotta go now, Girl

I'm really getting sleepy and lazy

Hebrews 3:15; Ephesians 5:14

That's alright Girlfriend, I can read your mind

I know you think that I'm going crazy

Acts 26:24,25

But wait a minute before you go Girlfriend

Let us call on Jesus' name

Isaiah 65:24

I'll make you a guarantee

That your life will never be the same

Romans 4:21; John 3:33

O. K. Help me, Girl

To confess, I really just don't know how

James 5:16; Romans 10:9,10

It's very simple, Girlfriend

Be open, and say, "God I want you now"

Isaiah 45:22; John 1:12

………………..

Girl, I'm so glad I stayed and prayed with you

My soul is so satisfied that I don't know what to do!

Psalms 103:1; Psalms 107:9

I felt a sweet sensation going down my back

I can see things clearly now, not dull nor black

Genesis 1:2; Proverbs 25:4

You know, Girlfriend

Huh, you're sounding just like me

Romans 8:16

That's alright Girlfriend

I've got Jesus, "Can't you see!"

Acts 2:2; Acts 4:31

I'm so glad I stopped by here tonight

Thanks so much for helping me see the light

Acts 9:18; John 5:30

That's what I've been trying to tell you Girlfriend

HE'S ALRIGHT!

Isaiah 55:11; 1 Corinthians 4:20; Psalms 115:3

Love reigns supreme and reality always rules.

AIN'T GOD GOOD!

Isaiah 45:2

How can you walk around

With that big, bright smile on your face?

Romans 8:31; 1 John 4:4

The way they've treated you Girlfriend

Huh, it's just a low down disgrace!

Psalms 34:19; Job 13:15

And how can you forgive them

For all the dishonorable things they've done?

Luke 6:37

And haven't you forgotten

Christina Abby

You lost your beloved son?

John 11:25; John 4:53

Haven't you heard the talk lately, Girlfriend?

They're mean and horrible things they say

John 21:20-22

It just couldn't be me Girlfriend

Hell, I'd just come in and GO OFF one day!

Acts 20:24

Girl, aren't you tired of working for nothing?

I'd ask them for much more pay

1 Timothy 5:18; Luke 10:2

And Girlfriend if they didn't accommodate my wishes

Shucks, I'd just pack up and be on my way!

100

Psalms 46:10; Psalms 27:14

You're extremely good Girlfriend

You've more control than me

Galatians 5:22,23

Cuz you just keep going and smiling

How, I just can't see!

Nehemiah 8:10

How do you do it, Girlfriend?

A lot of patience you've really got

Romans 5:3,4,5; Luke 21:19

I just don't understand it Girlfriend

You're definitely the woman that I'm not!

Proverbs 2:6; John 6:45

Christina Abby

Talk to me Girlfriend

Tell me your secret, I sure wish that you would

Psalms 25:14; Luke 8:11

You won't be misquoted

Nor misunderstood

Mark 4:14

Reflective of my past, Homegirl

I always wished that I could

Psalms 119:59; Isaiah 43:18,19

Now all I can say is……..

AIN'T GOD GOOD!

Psalms 84:11; Psalms 34:8

Know thy Self. Love thy Self. Respect thy Self. And let thy Self go to work for thy self.

<u>WHO IS HE?</u>

John 4:26

Who is this man that takes control

Replenishing, satisfying both body and soul?

John 7:38; Psalms 107:9

Extending His love, divine, I'm sure

Blessed is He whose heart is pure

John 9:32,33

WHO IS HE?

John 8:12

Who is this man that supplies each need

Displaying unselfishness toward color, nor creed

John 1:12; Acts 10:34

Touching our bodies that we may awake

Dying on Calvary's cross for all our sins' sake

John 1:29

WHO IS HE?

John 14:9

Who is this man that cannot lie

His mouth trangresseth not in judgment, no alibi

Luke 21:33; Psalms 89:34,35

Firm foundation, yet gentle with power galore

What riches and wealth is promised in store!

1 Corinthians 2:9

WHO IS HE?

John 10:7,9

Having sinned not

Yet willing to die

John 15:13; John 10:17,18

COME, THINK, LOOK, LISTEN

Can't you hear Mary cry?

John 20:11-15

WHO IS HE?

John 11:25

He needs no introduction if you are a saint

His name is Jesus in case you ain't!

Isaiah 9:6; Isaiah 4:14

King, Lord, Jehovah, to God be the glory

Please be attentive while I share my story

John 4:29; John 12:28

He picked me up one gray, gloomy day

To re-inform me of His righteous way

Deuteronomy 8:1-3

He said, "I AM the Way, Truth and the Life"

He relieved me of all my sorrows, my toils, my strifes

Mark 14:62; Mark 6:31

He gave me sweet, sweet love

In abundance untold

Ephesians 3:20

And filled my heart with joy, laughter

Praise be to Him, THANK GOD, I'm whole!

Psalms 45:1; Psalms 144:9

He wrapped His arms around me

"I love you, Chris"

Romans 8:38,39; 1 John 4:8

Come share my world of eternal bliss

Isaiah 27:3

He delivered me from Satan's highway of lies and deceit

He said, "Come, please come, I know no defeat!"

Exodus 3:14; Isaiah 45:7,22

Your arms are too short to box with God!

A land He promised that flows milk and honey

No bounced checks, I've plenty of money!

Luke 15:31

Christian Alan is safely wrapped in my bosom

So fret not, "Please don't despair"

Luke 8:52

It's you, your heart, Chris

That I'd like to repair

Matthew 5:8; Proverbs 4:23

Needless to say, but to no avail

Accountable AM I, my words won't fail

Matthew 4:4

If only you would

TRUST

Proverbs 3:5,6; Psalms 37:3-5

BELIEVE

Mark 9:23; Matthew 8:13

And **PRAY**

1 Thessalonians 5:15; Philippians 4:6,7

My kingdom and your child can be claimed

TODAY

Psalms 2:7,8; Luke 23:42,43; Luke 4:21; Luke 19:9

It is finished!

Mark 4:41; Luke 9:18-20

Principle, not personality.

TEARIN' UP A CHURCH

Jeremiah 33:3; Luke 4:36

Tain't no siddified folk

Gon' keep me in no lurch

1 Thessalonians 5:19; Ephesians 4:30

Come on in heh Holy Spirit

Let's tear up dis church!

And suddenly there came a sound from heaven as of a rushing mighty wind, and it filled the whole house where they were sitting.

Elaine jumped up

She couldn't stay down

Jeremiah 20:9; Hebrews 12:29

Done dashed up the aisle

Befo' I could turn around

Hebrews 4:12; Acts 5:39

Ruthie was spinning

As though in a trance

2 Corinthians 12:2-4

GOOD GOD A'MIGHTY!

I didn't know she could dance

Psalms 30:11; Ecclesiastes 3:1,4

Lisa was flailing

Hitting evahthang in reach

2 Corinthians 3:17; John 11:44

Shouting over and over

Preach, Holy Spirit, Teach!

John 14:16,17,26; Matthew 10:19,20

Carolyn was moaning and groaning

And just waving her hand

Romans 8:22,23; John 16:21,21

Lawd, give us wisdom

We don't understand

Proverbs 4:7; James 1:5,6

The Spirit twuz moving

It twuzn't hard to detect

Genesis 1:2; Joel 2:28-30

They were dancing like David

And it had a domino effect

2 Samuel 6:16; Acts 2:4-13

And God was rebuking non-believers

This ain't no game

Romans 3:3

"The Christ is the King of Glory"

Father, glorify Thy name!

John 12:28; Psalms 115:3

He'll show up and He'll show the hell out!

Proliferation is a mere byproduct of sanctification.

Christina Abby

THE KING'S HIGHWAY

Luke 14:21-23

I met a hitchhiker

Can I have a ride?

Hebrews 13:1-3; Philippians 2:3-5

Where are you going?

To the other side

Mark 4:35

I'm glad you picked me up

I have no place to go

Luke 10:33-37

I've lost my way

And I've been running to and fro

Luke 9:58

I've been beaten and thrown out

And a needed some space

Matthew 21:35,36; Luke 23:31

I've packed up my bags

And I'm looking for a new place

Hebrews 11:14,15

Have you been driving long

Why not take a rest?

Matthew 11:28-30; Mark 6:31

I've got a long way to go

I wanna see the crest

Philippians 3:13,14

You don't seem hurried though

Won't you be late?

Luke 21:19; Ecclesiastes 9:11

Where are you going?

To see the Golden Gate

Revelation 21:1-5

Oh, California

I've heard a lot about it

John 1:5; John 12:16

I've always wanted to go

How to get there, I really don't know

John 6:45

Postcard I got

Beautiful, you understand

Proverbs 29:18

Glorious, picturesque

Drawn by a Master's hand

Revelation 4:2-11; Psalms 89:6,7

Well, this is my stop

I really don't wanna get out

John 1:39,43; Luke 9:62

What can I do or say?

Acts 16:29,30; John 19:30

Come, Come along with me

I'm going that Way

John 14:6; John 10:7-9

Christina Abby

A friend in need needs a Friend indeed.

AN ATTITUDE OF GRATITUDE

Psalms 100

Simple Simon, the neighborhood lunatic

Trials of life have driven him mad

Psalms 91

Lord, we appreciate the lil' sense we've got

It's limited, but it ain't that bad

Psalms 34

Sistah Parker, the faithful, afflicted servant

Broken down body, racking with pain

Psalms 89

Lord, we're satisfied with our portion of health and strength

119

God forbid, if we ever complain

Psalms 107

Unlucky Larry, the confused, unsettled spirit

Just drinking and drugging his life away

Psalms 4

Lord, it could've been any of us struggling like that

Much obliged is what we really wanna say

Psalms 63

Sad Sunny, the fragile and battered soul

Put downs and beatings is all she seem to get

Psalms 119

Lord, we praise You for delivering us

And we haven't forgotten the things You've done for us yet

Psalms 124

You spared our minds, bodies, and souls

Our lot sure could've been worst

Psalms 66

Lord, You know Mamie's mom died last week

Either one of us couldn't been in that hearse

Psalms 150

Lord, I know we act proud and ungrateful sometimes

But we do understand that we ain't immuned

Psalms 131

We THANK YOU, THANK YOU right here and now

For speaking to our hearts and keeping us attuned

Psalms 45

Christina Abby

The crossroads is where the mind and the soul connect.

Christina Abby

THE THINKER

Psalms 119:15; Psalms 19:14

Now if you beget a son

Whatever is yours is also his

....

And she came to herself.

By heritage she's gone claim her portion

Now that's just the way it is!

I believe I'll make me a world.

Likewise, if Jesus is the daughter of God

Then she has dibs to the Father's whom she represents

And she girded up the loins of her mind.

So, in turn, Her daughters are due an inheritance too

124

Isn't that the reason why She was truly sent?

In Her was light and the light was the light of men.

If Jesus is the Father's representative

And the Father is One with Her Son

And the Spirit of God moved.

And you've been begotten by the Christ

Don't that make you and the Father also One?

This is my beloved daughter in whom I am well pleased.

And if you are One with the Father

Then you were there in the beginning too, it would appear

Arise and shine for thy light has come and the glory of the Lord has risen upon thee!

So that makes you a messenger just like Jesus

Can I get a WITNESS up in here?

This little light of mine, I'm gonna let it shine.

And if you were a witness from the beginning

Since you came from Jesus' flesh and bone

I of myself can do nothing but the Father doeth the work.

Then that makes you the I AM that I AM too

So indeed this world ain't none of your home

It is as you say.

And if you are One with the I AM that I AM

Then you're directly connected to God, the Father, the Queen

As you have believed, let it be unto you.

So why would you wanna live and act like a oppressed,
disenfranchised pauper

When by birthright you can have and do anything?

It is finished!

Psalms 82:6,7; 1 Timothy 4:15

And when God saw what she had made, she said: "Now, that's good!"

Contemplation always births revelation. As a woman thinketh in her heart so is she.

GOD'S PROPERTY

Isaiah 43:21; Jeremiah 1:4-7

Filly, where did you get that car? Oh, my Daddy saw fit that I could

have it. And guess what, Girl, He made sure that I got a raise on my

job too! He's sooo good to me! He stopped by here this morning,

touched me with His finger of love, put activity in my limbs, clothed

me in my right mind and started me on my way. I'm gonna praise

Him. HALLELUJAH! I'm gonna praise Him!

Luke 11:2; Psalms 104:30

Girl, I sure do like what you've done to this place. Thanks, me too,

Girl. My Daddy is sooo good to me. HOSANNA! I'm gonna praise

Him. I told them boys that in this house, we're gonna praise my

Daddy. He sure is worthy!

Joshua 24:15; Psalms 89:6,7

Are you going to revival tonight, Girl? Yes, I shole am, Girl. If I

don't, I might miss my blessings. Girl, when you start praising my

Daddy, tain't no telling what might happen! So I'm gonna praise Him.

HALLELUJAH! I'm gonna praise Him. HOSANNA to the

HIGHEST! I'm gonna praise Him.

Hebrews 6:14; Acts 16:25,26

I'm gonna praise Him morning, noon, and evening

I'm gonna praise Him in and out of season

1 Corinthians 6:20

GLORY!

John 12:28; Revelation 4:11

Him waking me up this morning

Is a mighty, mighty good reason!

Psalms 150:6

I'm gonna praise Him, ALLELUIA

Christina Abby

Revelation 19:1-3,6

I'm gonna praise Him, GLORY!

I'm gonna praise Him

GLORY HALLELUJAH!

Mark 11:9,10; Psalms 79:13

Let the redeemed of the Lord say so whom He has redeemed from the hand of the enemy.

<u>SIMPLY PROFOUND</u>

Mark 4:26-32

If you've only had *consciousness* of night

How would you *evaluate* when it was day?

Psalms 19:1,2; Psalms 30:5

And if you never had an *awareness* otherwise

How could you *conceive* something another way?

Luke 24:45

If you've never *recognized* rain

How would you *translate* a rainbow?

Genesis 9:15,16

And if you've never *observed* life in action

Christina Abby

How would you *grasp* the concept sow and grow?

Mark 4:26-28; 1 Corinthians 3:9

If you've never been *engulfed* in chaos

How would you *assess* when it was quiet and still?

Isaiah 30:15; 1 Corinthians 14:33

And if you've never *believed* anything or anyone

How could you *ascertain* if they won't or they will?

Matthew 8:13; John 11:40

If you've never *developed* convictions

How would you *reconcile* when to agree or disagree?

Daniel 3:17,18; Amos 3:3

And if you've never had *insight* into bondage

What would be your *interpretation* of being free?

132

Acts 3:4-8; Luke 17:15,16; John 11:44; John 5:6-8

If you've never had *knowledge* of options

How would you *determine* how and when to make a choice?

Psalms 119:59; Luke 15:17,18; Joshua 24:15

And if you never opened your mouth

How would you or anybody else *know* that you had a voice?

2 Peter 2:16; Psalms 77:16-20; 1 Kings 19:11-13

If you never *listened* to anything or anyone

How could anyone *confirm* that you could even hear?

1 Samuel 3:9; 1 Kings 19:11-13

If you've never *displayed* courage

What could or would you *define* fear?

Romans 8:15; Mark 4:40

If you've never *savored* the sweetness of life

How could *pronounce* something good or bad?

Psalms 34:8; Revelation 10:8-10

And if you never *experienced* happiness

What would be your *perception* of sad?

Galatians 5:22,23; John 11:32

If you've never been on the outside

How would you *know* to appreciate when you were really in?

John 9:25; Acts 4:19,20

And if you've never really begun anything

How could you even give *consideration* to a potential end?

Isaiah 43:18,19; Revelation 21:2-5

If you've never *embraced* anything

How could you *convey* when and what you feel

Luke 24:32; 1 Corinthians 2:10

And if you've never *pondered* truth

How would you *know* that what you *thought* you *thought* was really really real?

Proverbs 16:3; Proverbs 23:7

If you've never been through anything

What would be your *revelation* of going through?

Psalms 23:4; Proverbs 24:16

And if you never *tested* an hypothesis

How could you *verify* your findings false or true?

John 6:45

The majestic oak is inside of a puny old seed.

THE PRAYING MANTIS

Psalms 46:10; Isaiah 40:31

Des folks jus' keep on botherin' me

Dey prob'ly ben messin' wit you too

John 10:10; 1 Peter 5:8

I had done tole dey had best leave me be

Now I know 'xactly what I'm gon' hafta do!

Psalms 4:4

First, I bought me dis heh helmet

Cuz dey wuz jus' tanklin' wit my head

Isaiah 26:3; James 2:19

Dat proved wasteful and ineffective

Cuz den dey attacked my heart instead

Proverbs 4:23

Den I bought me dis heh breastplate

You know I had to preserve my tender heart

Psalms 19:14; Matthew 5:8

Dem stab wombs got so deep and vicious

Dat thang jus' broke down and fell apart!!

Job 1:7; Job 2:7

After dat, I bought me som' boxin' gloves

I said, COME ON, BRANG IT ON, I'm gon' give you a real good
fight

Revelation 13:10; Romans 12:21

De mo' I b'gan to thank 'bout dat idear

Sumthin' in my Spirit jus' didn't sat right

Romans 8:22,26; John 11:33

I'm now workin' on gittin' me one of dem whole armors

Dat solid kind dat you jus' can't penetrate

Ephesians 6:11-13

I'm gon' beat dem down bad den, you watch and see

Oooooh, I'm jus' so 'xcited

I can't hardly wait!

Psalms 138:8; Psalms 89:22,23

Meanwhile, I'm gon' git me som' knee pads

Cuz I be knowing how to protect me and mines

Philippians 4:6,7; Psalms 91:4

PRAYING is the most potent weapon dat I know

Huh, like Colt 45, it works e'vry time!

1 Chronicles 4:10; Psalms 78:65,66

In a paradoxical manner, silence is never silent. Still waters run deep.

STAYING ON THE PORCH

Psalms 127:1,2

Sitting out on Solomon's porch

Just talking and laughing on hot Mississippi day

2 Chronicles 1:10-12

Mystified by the stuff he told me

Now this is what he had to say

1 Corinthians 2:14; 2 Corinthians 5:1

You ought to build you a big ole house

And I know the perfect builder to call

1 Corinthians 3:10-14; Psalms 11:3

You'll be so pleased when He's finished, Child

I guarantee you won't be disappointed at all

Jeremiah 29:11-14; Acts 7:47-50

Now you want certain things in your house

I believe I know what's good for you

Psalms 84:11; Philippians 2:13

Listen real closely, my Child

I'm gonna tell you exactly what you need to do

Psalms 45:10

First and foremost, you've gotta get a storehouse call wisdom

And make sure you get a room for understanding too

Proverbs 4:7; James 1:5,6

Add a lotta space for grace and mercy

Child, He'll be elated to do that for you

Psalms 89:14; Psalms 145:8,9

Make sure you get an upper room

So you can bow down and meditate

Philippians 4:8; 1 Timothy 4:15

And don't forget a room for compassion

So people in need can come and congregate

Lamentations 3:22; Luke 10:33,37; Hosea 6:6

Also, build you an extra large room called faith

Now, that's a room you just can't live without

Galatians 3:6; Hebrews 11:1,6

Then get yourself another room for unconditional love

And you'll have something beautiful, tain't no doubt!

Romans 13:10; 1 Corinthians 13:1-13

Finally, get a receptive, inviting guest room

So that the builder can move in with you

Isaiah 6:8; Revelation 3:20

Now if you really want to be safe and secure

That's something you've just gotta do

Psalms 62:2; Psalms 91:1-4

SKIT, SKAT, RUN

Go give Him a ring

Nehemiah 2:17,18

Time is perpetually, eternally fleeting

We've got to start building this thing!

Luke 6:47,48

And he huffed and he puffed and he couldn't blow it down.

<u>AMAZING GRACE</u>

John 15:16; Luke 19:34

Saul, Saul

Why are you persecuting Me?

Job 38:4; John 16:33

I'm the Creator of the universe

And there's nothing I can't do nor see

John 1:1-3; Proverbs 15:3

I know all about you

Whether you've ever been told

John 2:25; Jeremiah 1:5

My kingdom will come

And you can't kick against the goads!

Luke 11:2-4; Acts 9:5

It's time for a change, Saul

The gospel you can no longer pervert

Acts 13:10; 1 Corinthians 15:51-54

Enough is Enough!

You're now under blinding light alert

John 9:39-41

Get up, keep on traveling

Ananias is who you're gonna meet

Acts 9:10

You'll know exactly who he is

He'll be on the corner of Crooked and Straight Streets

Acts 9:11; John 1:23; Isaiah 40:4

Shut up, Ananais!

Romans 11:18; Matthew 20:14,15

Just do as I say

And give him back his sight

Psalms 119:91; John 10:27

Just touch his eyes, Ananais

I want him to see crystal clear today

Acts 9:17,18; Mark 8:22-25

You're going to hafta suffer, Paul

All for my name's sake

Psalms 34:19; 2 Corinthians 11:24-27

Don't be too concerned about it

It's just something you're going to hafta take

Acts 20:23,24; 2 Corinthian 4:8-10

You're My vessel now

According to My Father's will

2 Corinthians 4:7; Matthew 22:14

I'm still on the throne, Paul

So, "Peace Be Still"

Mark 4:35-39; John 14:27

Pick up your cross, Paul

Because I want you to shine for Me

Acts 13:47; Matthew 5:16

There's plenty of work to be done

Come, Come, and See

Luke 14:21-23; Luke 10:2,3

Christina Abby

Simply profound. Underneath the skin, everything and everybody is kin.

EXTRA! EXTRA! READ ALL ABOUT IT!

Proverbs 25:2

EXTRA! EXTRA

I think you should know

If you had the savior, Jesus

Lies and deceit would automatically go

John 5:39

He did die

But yet He arose

Acts 13:30; Psalms 85:11

READ FOR YOURSELF

It's not written in prose

Psalm 119:105; Romans 11:33; Psalms 147:5

Readily available

For all men to obtain

John 1:12; John 6:37

With wars and destruction around us

How can we sustain?

Psalms 124:1,2; Psalms 11:3

He is the rock of redemption

Both Faithful and True

Revelation 19:11; Psalms 89:34,35

What He says, "BANK ON IT"

He won't fail you

Luke 4:4; Isaiah 55:11; Hebrews 6:18

The BIBLE is the Way

To eternity and preservation

Psalms 1:1-6; Mark 4:14

Pick it up

And review the divine revelation

Psalms 111:2

He is love, the moon and the sun

Possibilities are endless, including life, joy and fun

Galatians 5:22,23

Happiness, excellence, brilliance

All found in He

Revelation 19:12-16; Isaiah 41:4

Life without Him

How miserable you must be!

John 15:1-6

He carried all of our sins

Laid down on His back

John 1:29; Romans 5:6-8

A very heavy burden, I might add

But given no slack

Luke 23:34

He did it for all

Not Hispanics, Jews, Whites nor Blacks

Romans 2:11; Galatians 3:26-29

SAVE YOURSELF!

God knows, He's coming back

John 14:2,3

He suffered at Calvary

For all men to see

John 12:32

Not for Himself

But for sinners, like you, you and me

Romans 3:23; Romans 5:6-8

Led like a lamb to be slaughtered

Not a word He spake

John 10:18

Humble, though powerful

How much can He take?

Mark 14:36

They threw rocks

And laughed out loud

Acts 3:17

Pierced in the side

Consistently ridiculed by the crowd

Luke 22:63,64; John 19:2-5

Nailed to the cross

Both hands and feet

Luke 18:32,33; Job 13:15

PICTURE THIS:

A sharp instrument in your meat!

Matthew 27:33-35

King or Lord of the Jews

The inscription boldly read

Luke 22:70; Luke 23:38

Mute to it all

Not a word He said

John 19:9

SAVE YOURSELF!

Should you be the deliverer?

Mark 15:30,31; Luke 23:39

If they only knew

Hearts, minds, and souls would quiver

Psalms 73:22; Luke 23:34; Acts 7:60

He finally succumbed

And gave up the Ghost

155

Luke 23:46; Psalms 31:5

I'm glad I found Him

He's worthy to boast

Psalms 34:1,4; Psalms 103:1,2

I have many, many treasures

Put away for me

John 14:2,3; 1 Corinthians 2:9

Jewels so precious

The spiritually blind can't see

1 Corinthians 2:14; John 9:39-41

If you would like more

Enlightenment of the same

James 1:5,6; 2 Chronicles 1:10-12

Just call Him up

The Christ is His name

Jeremiah 33:3; Isaiah 65:24

Words from the Bible

Peace, joy, love, wisdom, salvation, being FREE

Ephesians 4:7,8

EXTRA! EXTRA! EXTRA!

He gave it all to me!

Psalms 12:6

*If you don't sow anything, you certainly won't grow anything. A
Bible that's falling apart reveals a saint who ain't.*

Christina Abby

<u>NIP IT IN THE BUD</u>

Ephesians 6:11-13

She buffaloed Sandra

And intimidated Lou

1 Peter 5:8; Job 1:6,7

She manipulated Paul

What were they to do?

Genesis 3:1-5

She intimidated Tina

And railroaded Grace

John 10:10

She bamboozled Rose

And got all up in her face

Luke 4:1-12; John 8:44

In comes Alan

What can I say?

Acts 5:3,4, Acts 13:10

She disrespected him

In her utmost way!

Job 2:7

He swallowed his pride

And then let it go

Romans 12:21; Mark 14:36,38

She got away again

Say it ain't so!

Galatians 6:7; Psalms 37:13

Two weeks later

She chose to stop by

1 Corinthians 15:33; Luke 4:13

I'll do it again

At least I'm gone try

Luke 23:31; 1 Corinthians 10:13

I can read your mind

So don't you even try

1 Peter 3:15; Proverbs 15:1

I've peeped your hole card

And I know your modus operandi

John 8:32,36; James 4:7

You've done this stuff

Too many times before

1 Peter 5:8; Romans 12:17-18

Now, I'm telling you nicely

Don't do that anymore

Ephesians 4:26-28; James 3:17,18

What you don't address will inevitably cause you stress.

Christina Abby

THE SOULS OF COMMON FOLK

Acts 10:15

Ms. Cora Bea attends church evah Sunday

Kneels, give thanks when she pray

Philippians 4:6

Takes care of six grands

A God-fearing woman, I hafta say

Matthew 5:16

Ms. Beulah volunteers at the nursing home

Never heard her once complain

Acts 9:6; Isaiah 6:8

Lawd, they're expecting me today

Protect me from harm's way out in this rain

Isaiah 54:17

Mr. Nicodemus drives folk to the field

GOD BLESS YOU, he says to everyone

John 3:1-5; Luke 10:27

Lord, I need to get them some hats

They need a covering from this blazing sun

Acts 12:8; Revelation 19:13

Ms. Annie Mae waits on the porch

Just grinning about God's mercy and grace

Psalms 124:1

Beulah Chile, it won't be long fo' my homegoing

I can taste and see my new place

Psalms 34:8; Psalms 25:14

I heard them streets are so nice

And I believe what I've been told

Matthew 8:13; John 7:38

Nicodemus! Nicodemus, aint gone be no mud there

Man, them streets are lined wit gold!

Revelation 4:2-6; Revelation 21:14-21

And Cora Bea, there won't be no doctor bills either

For your chilluns' scrapes and colds

Isaiah 53:5; Revelation 22:1,2

Beulah, you won't need that Dark and Lovely either

Honey Chile, cuz we ain't gone ever grow old!

Psalms 92:11-14; Psalms 91:16

Its all a matter of consciousness.

BASS ACKWARDS

Job 38:2

There's a whole world out there

And I'm gonna claim whatever is mine

Psalms 24:1

Give me my portion right now

And you had better come through this time!

Isaiah 29:16

Let me see one of Your so-called miracles

The ones other folk are talking about

Lamentations 3:22,23

Prove me wrong now herewith

Or else go ahead and work my problems out!

Psalms 78:20

You ain't so gracious anyhow

And I've never ask you for no break

Luke 6:35

If seeing is truly believing

Then Your credibility is surely at stake

Psalms 94:8-11

I'm sick of Your spiritual fanatics

Scientific detail has proven them wrong

Job 38:31-38

I just wanna confirm my findings one more time

Then I'mma leave You and your crackpots alone!

167

Christina Abby

Psalms 139:7,8

I'm giving You one more chance

And I already know you ain't gonna come through

Matthew 8:13

Frankly, I don't care one way or the other

Because I ain't a believer in You!

John 6:64; Romans 3:3

Order or Chaos? Reality or Rhetoric? Victim or Victor? Truth or
Consequence?

BACK TO THE BASICS

Matthew 7:7,8

Assign, align me in Your awareness

Luke 24:45

Beget, bless me in Your blessedness

Psalms 2:7,8; Hebrews 6:14

Comfort, cleanse me in Your clarity

John 14:18; Proverbs 25:4

Discipline, delight me in Your deliverance

Revelation 3:18,19; Isaiah 48:10

Enrich, enrapture me in Your enlightenment

Colossians 1:26,27

Feed, fill me in Your faithfulness

Psalms 37:3-5

Ground, guide me in Your godliness

Psalms 32:8,9; Psalms 73:24

Humble, heal me in Your holiness

Hebrews 5:8; Jeremiah 8:22

Inspire, instruct me in Your intellect

Hebrews 9:8-12; Psalms 147:5

Judge, justify me in Your justice

Romans 5:9,10

Kindle, keep me in Your kindness

Isaiah 27:3; Psalms 103:8-10

Leaven, lavish me in Your love

Romans 8:38,39

Mold, maintain me in Your munificence

Jeremiah 29:11-14

Nurture, nourish me in Your nature

John 13:16; Luke 6:40

Open, order me in Your omniscience

Psalms 37:23,31

Purge, prune me in Your perfection

Psalms 51:7; Psalms 138:8

Quantify, quicken me in Your qualities

Genesis 2:7; Hebrews 4:12

Remember, revive me in Your righteousness

Genesis 9:15,16

Satisfy, sustain me in Your sufficiency

2 Corinthians 3:5,6; 2 Corinthians 12:9

Teach, transform me in Your truth

John 6:45; John 17:17

Use, usher me in Your understanding

Luke 19:34; Proverbs 3:5,6

Validate, value me in Your virtue

John 1:12; Matthew 3:17

Wash, water me in Your wisdom

Isaiah 1:18; Proverbs 2:6

Xamine me

Psalms 26:2

Yoke me in Your yearning

John 4:23,24; Luke 9:56

Zap me in Your zeal

John 3:27; Philippians 2:13

Fundamentally, information is just like money.
You can't spend It unless you've got It.

Christina Abby

I AM DIVINE

Luke 15:31; Isaiah 60:1

I AM Mother/Father Earth

I have the capacity to fertilize and conceive

I AM the contemplative, consummate thinker

I can creatively manifest what I think, know, and believe

This little light of mine, I'm gonna let it shine.

I AM mysteriously clairvoyant

The soul of my soul has an eye

I AM perpetual eternality

I know the who, what, when, how where, and the why

This little light of mine, I'm gonna let it shine.

I AM the crisp, refreshing breath of life

The embodiment of wisdom: the kaleidoscopic effervescence of an
ocean blue

I AM the tones, shapes, rhythms and colors of existence

The visual hues of both old and new

This little light of mine, I'm gonna let it shine.

I AM simply amazing grace

The epitome of peace, elegance, love, and joy

I AM universality expressed in individuality

The hopes and dreams of every man, woman, girl and boy

This little light of mine, I'm gonna let it shine.

I AM the Truth, the whole Truth, and nothing but the Truth

And I cannot/will not compromise

I AM the perceptively powerful eagle; the phoenix

175

I can soar high, higher: Still I rise. I rise.

This little light of mine, I'm gonna let it shine.

I AM the Master's ideal concept

A perfectly framed replica of the Mind of minds

I AM the Word in all of its infinity

Therefore, phenomenally, intrinsically so

I AM DIVINE

John 1:14; Amos 3:3

"Rejoice, O barren,

You who do not bear!

Break forth and shout,

You who do not travail!

For the desolate has many more children

Than she who has husband."

Galatians 4:27

176

Let it shine. Let it shine. Let it shine.

Sojourn in this truth. The birth pangs and delivery of a people moan, groan, and echo loudly, deeply, persistently in the heart and mind of a fertile belly: the womb of a certain woman's soul.

Christina Abby

<u>THE JOURNEY</u>

Luke 9:58

Sailing the waters of life

Gliding over turbulent space

John 16:33

Yearning for peace, comfort, stability

In relentless pursuit of my place

Psalms 42:1,2

Navigating aimlessly, recklessly

Obsessing, possessing things along the way

John 6:27

Disillusioned by their emptiness

Oh, the price I've had to pay

Mark 8:36

Searching, starving for fulfillment

A mysteriously magnetic pull begins

Luke 8:46-48; 2 Corinthians 10:4,5

The tides are rising rapidly now

I believe its time to go back in

Mark 6:31; Hebrews 6:19,20

All roads ultimately lead back to the Father's house.

Christina Abby

<u>THE LOADED WEAPON</u>

Proverbs 18:21

Flipping and flopping

Splishing and splashing

James 3:8

Yipping and yapping

Spewing and lashing

Proverbs 21:23

Vulgar and venomous

Sharp and crude

Proverbs 10:31

Cutting and unbridled

Insensitive and rude

James 1:26

Attacking and slanderous

Haughty and proud

Proverbs 6:17

Maliciously nasty

Cocky and loud

Proverbs 15:1

Brutish and piercing

Harsh and mean

Proverbs 21:23

Crooked and criminal

Terse and obscene

John 19:10

Callous and ill-tempered

Brazenly bold

Proverbs 25:23

Dangerous deadly

When it's out of control

Proverbs 29:11; Proverbs 17:27,28

Loose lips sink ships. Today, beginning right now, I will consciously open my mind before I open my mouth.

<u>GOD, WE AIN'T</u>

John 1:3; Psalms 89:6,7

You ain't my master

And I ain't your slave

Romans 11:18; 1 Corinthians 4:7

You can't control my actions

And I ain't gone behave

Ephesians 6:11-13

You ain't the King of Kings

I ain't no sinner

John 1:29; John 15:2

You can't predestine my life

And I can't pick the winners

Isaiah 45:7,22

You can't buy my soul

And I ain't for sale

Proverbs 23:23; 1 Corinthians 6:20

You can't lock me up in misery

And I ain't got no bail

2 Corinthians 3:17; Acts 16:25,26

You can't trot on my heart

And I ain't made of glass

Proverbs 4:23; Psalms 19:14

You ain't no astrologer

And I haven't forgotten the past

Hebrews 8:12; Genesis 9:15,16; Psalms 103:11-14

You can't select my home

And I ain't living where I'd like

Joshua 24:15; Luke 23:42,43

You can't drive my Toyota

And I ain't got no bike

Luke 15:31

You can't love me anymore

And I ain't in love

Romans 13:10; 1 Corinthians 13:1,13

You ain't no eagle

And I ain't no dove

Matthew 3:17; Exodus 3:14

You can't be so pure

And I ain't that defiled

2 Corinthians 10:12

You can't be that forgetful

And I'm definitely not senile

Isaiah 17:10,11; Hebrews 8:8-12

What's the difference?

You say you can

Matthew 5:25

Lord knows I can't

One thing we oughta agree on

GOD, WE AIN'T

2 Timothy 2:23; 1 Timothy 3:16

When you can agree to disagree agreeably, then you'll always be in agreement.

<u>MARY, MARY, DON'T YOU WEEP</u>

Luke 10:42

Conceived in the back seat of a car

Parents got married. That just what they had to do

Proverbs 18:10

Didn't know what love, adulthood, or life was all about

Rose to the occasion for their adorable baby, YOU

Mark 12:44

Prayed, taught, nurtured and loved you

Showered you with gifts, even when they went without

1 Thessalonians 5:17

"Rob Peter to pay Paul;" "Rob Peter to pay Paul"

You never understood what that was all about

Galatians 3:6

Happy go lucky, well adjusted child you were

No problems, cares or concerns

Matthew 6:34; 1 Peter 5:7

Mama was extremely rich in Spirit, yet poor

No one the wiser could ever discern

Proverbs 28:11; James 2:5

Went to prayer meeting and regular service every Sunday

Just because you wanted to, you see

Psalms 107:9; Psalms 34:8

Taught the importance of prayer and thanksgiving

Loved the comfort the Church provided me

Christina Abby

Proverbs 1:8; Proverbs 22:6

Got involved in church-related activities

Cultivated friendships and an extended family too

Acts 18:9,10; Hebrews 12:2

Envisioned a life of peace and prosperity

Get me an education; that's what I've gotta do!

Psalms 37:3,4,5; Philippians 4:8

Attended the 'private, white-folk' high school

At Mama's, the minister and community's expense

Philippians 2:3,4

Got exposed to *Browning, Emerson, Homer, Tennyson, Whitman, and Dante*

Milton's *Paradise Lost* now made some sense

Luke 15:13-32

Watched the comings and goings of the affluent

Emulated them – inquiring minds really, really wanna know

Psalms 8:4; Isaiah 2:22

Never invited to their parties was your question?

'Because you're Black'

Please, please, say it ain't so!

Luke 23:34; Acts 3:17

Didn't expect that kind of education

Confused, belief system and spiritual foundation rocked

Psalms 118:8,22-23; Proverbs 25:19

Transformed you into a bitter angry young man

Mama paid for counseling to help you overcome the shock

Psalms 4:4; Mark 14:38

191

Got encouragement from friends and foes alike

"Don't give up on that vision you have in view."

Isaiah 26:3; Romans 12:2

"Keep on going my sweet, sweet baby."

"Son, you've got to do what you've gotta do!"

John 2:5; John 5:6-8

Prayed incessantly about it

Pleaded with God for understanding and relief

Psalms 18:3; Jeremiah 33:3

Got a different perspective on the situation afterward

Licked my wounds and dug a hole for my grief!

Luke 18:7,8; Luke 17:19

Went to school each and every day

Tolerated my adversaries like they tolerated me

Matthew 5:25; Romans 12:21

Tunnel vision when it came to your studies

Education was the only way out: No apology

Proverbs 29:18; John 6:45

Graduation day: The substance of everything hoped for

That forever anticipated, joyous, exciting event

Romans 5:2-5; Colossians 1:26,27

Avoided and disowned your own Mama

She cried and even hated that she went

Luke 2:51

The whole community rallied around you

You just weren't comfortable around that simple, religious crowd

Proverbs 29:23; John 7:18

They were country folk who talked in broken English

And their clothes were cheap and loud

James 4:16; 1 Corinthians 4:7; Romans 11:18

Got yourself into "self-made" University

Ms. Johnson sure was a lot of help

Isaiah 17:10,11; 2 Chronicles 7:14

Made sure Mama wasn't involved in that process

Previous embarrassments had left too many whelps

Luke 2:19

Done moved on to the big city now

Transition and adjustment has been relatively smooth

Lamentations 3:22,23

You understand what is really, really important

"You've gotta, gotta get out of school"

Psalms 19:1,2

Didn't take long to become enamored with your freedom

Oh, that magnetic force of the bright city lights

2 Corinthians 11:14; John 7:24

Never responded to Mama's calls or letters

She should just assumed everything was alright

Hebrews 3:15; Malachi 2:10

You don't go to church anymore either

The sermons are weak and boring anyhow

Jeremiah 18:15

I don't believe in that shouting and emotional stuff

195

"Huh, I'm a bona fide, cultured, 'intellectual' now!"

Psalms 78:56-59; Psalms 50:22

You've done extremely well in school though

In fact, you'll get your doctorate in about a week

Deuteronomy 8:18

Mama sure would like to come

But an invitation is what she really seeks

Proverbs 13:12

She won't be getting one though

There just aren't enough to go around

Philippians 2:3,4

"She'll get over it," you say

"I'm hosting a dignitary from out of town"

John 12:43

Done opened up mine own practice now

Got married, and got me a baby that looks just like me

2 Corinthians 12:9

Business is thriving and I'm successful now

Gee, everything is going oh so well you see

Luke 4:5; 2 Corinthians 4:18

Built yourself a beautiful, palatial mansion

Hewn out of the most exclusive kind of granite and rock

Psalms 127:1, 2; Luke 7:49

You haven't been to see Mama in years

Gee, how time passes: tick tock, tick, tock

Revelation 3:20

She's never met your wife, or grandchildren

Daddy is dead on gone you see

Romans 10:21

"Shole wish I could see my only child," Mama says

"Lawd, please send my baby back to me"

Psalms 51:17; Luke 17:19; Proverbs 12:25

A racist act triggered some old memories

You *remembered* how your community helped you out befo'

Psalms 119:59,67,71

You thought you were protected from that kind of treatment

It truly, truly hurt, don't you know!

Psalms 91:1,9-12

Realized how mixed up you were

The more things change, the more they remain the same

Malachi 3:6; Psalms 119:89; Hebrews 13:8

The simple things in life seem important now

Success and honor can't bring you fame

Proverbs 15:33; James 4:6,10

You immediately phoned Mama up

"Mama, I truly want to make amends"

1 Corinthians 14:40; 1 John 1:9

"Can you please me for my foolishness"

"Lord, Mama, I wanna come back in"

Luke 15:17,18; Matthew 11:25

Mama told everybody about it

Oh, what a glorious revelation!

John 12:28

In spite of all of my shortcomings and amnesia

Everybody gladly attended the celebration

Proverbs 11:10

My wife, me and my chillun are back in the Church now

De way de peoples talk, dress and praise God

Don't bother me one darn bit!

1 Corinthians 6:20

In fact, I find myself walkin,' actin,' and talking,' lak 'em

Lest I evah wanna forgit!

Act 1:8; Acts 5:39

I already AM what I was searching for

In fact, I just finished reading Milton's *Paradise Regained*

Luke 23:42,43

I'm so glad to be back wit des religious country folk

I thank God and my Mama dey still treat me the same!

Isaiah 48:10; Psalms 103:11-14

Introspection, involution precedes evolution.

Christina Abby

DIVERSITY, INDIVIDUALITY IN

UNIVERSALITY

Deuteronomy 6:4; 1 Corinthians 12:13-27

You have praise and glory that I can't give

You have a human experience that I can't live

Psalms 19:34; Acts 13:47

You have a song that I don't know and I can't sing

You have an offering of gratitude that only you can bring

Luke 1:46

You have some dreams that I can't make come true

You're gonna have trials that only you can go through

Romans 8:18; John 11:4; Proverbs 25:4

You have many lessons that only you can learn

You're gonna get some stripes that only you can earn

John 6:45; Luke 12:47,48; John 16:33

You have hopes that I don't know and I can't fulfill

And you're bound to get some wounds that only God can heal

Jeremiah 8:22

You have a wonderful story that only you can tell

And I've got tests to pass that only I fail

Proverbs 24:16; Psalms 119:59,67,71

You're gonna shed some tears that only you can cry

And there's gonna be many questions but you won't know why?

Romans 11:33,34; Psalms 147:5

You have a battle that only you can fight

There are imperfections in all of us that neither of us can make right

Christina Abby

1 Chronicles 20:15,17; Psalms 138:8

You have goals and aspirations that only you can reach

And I've got a sermon that only I can't preach

Matthew 5:16

You have a purpose that I can't conceive nor believe

And you have a destiny that only you can achieve

Psalms 22:27,28; John 10:16

*To thine own Self be true. Each of us, individually, alone, must
unravel life's little riddle.*

PRIMAL PRE-EMINENCE

Psalms 104:30

"I've got a feeling everything gonna be alright. I just elevated my power to a higher level last night."

John 7:18

That's serious business, Girl

And there's no humor in it at all

Isaiah 17:10,11

I like you better down here

Come on down now before you fall

Proverbs 16:18

"I don't care what you say. I don't care what you think. I'm controlling these waters of life and I know my ship ain't gonna sink!"

Luke 14:11; Psalms 37:13

I'm gonna tell ya something

And I'm gonna be real frank

John 17:17

I thank you've gotten too big for your britches

Now that's what I truly thank!

Isaiah 14:10-14

"Yours too tight and you can't tell. And if you gonna keep trying to tell me what to do, you can go straight to hell!"

James 4:16; Romans 10:21

What I'm trying to say is

I think you've misinterpreted the key

Isaiah 29:16

You're entertaining some "strange" fruit

The same thing almost happened to me

2 Corinthians 11:14; John 8:32

"You can say whatever you like, but I'll never be the same. I know I'm on to something and there ain't no shame in my game."

Again, that serious, Girl

Come on back while you can

Isaiah 17:10,11

If you get too far out there

It's gonna be difficult to get back again

Matthew 13:28

"Don't you worry about me. I've got it all under control. You really need to mind your own business and run over your own shoe soles!"

John 3:19

O.K., I've warned you

When will you ever learn?

Deuteronomy 30:1-3

Christina Abby

When you keep playing with fire

You're certain to get burned

John 15:1-6

God is connected to man like the finger is to the hand.

THANKSGIVING BOULEVARD

Matthew 11:28-30

Heaven on earth

Residing on Lover's Lane

Luke 10:27

Soon moved to Divorce Court

Nearly drove me insane!

Luke 15:12,13

Right on to Single's Circle

Ended up on Disappointment Drive

John 6:27

Took some Dead End Cul de Sacs

Tired! Tired! Tired!

Mark 6:31; Psalms 37:7

Went on over to Independence Route

Catapulted me to Proud Avenue

James 4:6

Got evicted to Rejection Hill

Didn't know what I was gonna do!

James 3:16; Genesis 4:1-7; Isaiah 14:10-14

Ended up in Confusion Park

Took a sharp, sharp left down Bitter Row

Revelation 10:8,9

Still searching for an Easy Street

Don't ever wanna travel those roads no mo!

John 12:24

Came to a Lonely Highway

Stony the Road I had to trod

Mark 4:35

Came to a Place called Surrender Junction

Now, I live on Thanksgiving Boulevard

Luke 23:46; Psalms 31:5

Surrender is the highest form of exaltation. Beyond the valley of humiliation lies a fertile plateau.

<u>SWEEPING AROUND</u>

Proverbs 24:30-34

"God, you know I wanna be nice. But, Lord, this is an enormous sacrifice."

Girl, why didn't you call me back?

I knew you had guests

2 Thessalonians 3:11,12

But need to talk to you

Now ain't that a reasonable request?

Job 1:7

"Lord, have mercy. You know I don't want us to fall out. Why does she coming over here? What is this all about?"

1 Corinthians 15:33

Girl, I don't like my neighbors

They moved in the other night

Mark 12:31

Girl, I sense I'm gonna have problems with them

I can feel it, I know something ain't right

1 Corinthians 8:2

"Lord, Lord, Lord, her she comes again. What am I suppose to do? If she keep coming over here gossiping, Lord, I'm sorry, but she and I gone hafta be through.

Psalms 46:10

Girl, those folk across from me

There's just too much traffic over there

Romans 3:23

I'm gonna call the cops again

They'll be mad, but I don't care

Luke 6:41

"I'm sick of this now, Lord. Please, give me the words to say. I don't mean to hurry you but can't you do it for me today?"

Isaiah 65:24

Girl, look at their front yard

But Girl you oughta see the back

Proverbs 20:19

Doesn't it bother you some?

Girl, it's about to give me a heart attack!

Proverbs 15:33

I know they're breaking some laws

Girl, why don't you give the authorities a call?

Proverbs 2:11

I've called them too many times, I guess

Now they won't respond to me at all

Proverbs 4:31; Proverbs 4:16

Why are you grinning like that

Do you have something to say?

Proverbs 10:12

Go ahead and spit out

Cuz I don't like you looking at me that way

Zechariah 4:6

"Thank you, Lord! I've finally got my chance. You're so gracious and faithful. I believe I'll dance!"

I'm glad you asked

Yes, I do have something to say

Proverbs 17:27,28

Here's a piece of advice for you

Well, let me put it this way

James 3:17

You need to mind your own business

And leave other folk alone

John 8:7; Romans 3:23

You ain't got no business snooping and reporting

What's going on in other people homes

1 Peter 4:15; Psalms 75:7

Why are you so nosy anyhow?

I've asked you that time and time befo'

Proverbs 17:9

You've got a lotta dirt and debris in an out of your house

And you know I really know!

Isaiah 29:15

I don't want to hear anything negative

So don't come over her gossiping anymore

Proverbs 28:23; Philippians 4:8

First, get your own house in order

SWEEP AROUND YOUR OWN FRONT DOOR

1 Corinthians 14:40; Luke 6:41,42; Matthew 7:1-5

The enemy is within. Therefore, man's most formidable foe is his own ego.

Christina Abby

"THE WAYS"

To every man there openeth

A Way, and Ways, and a Way,

The High Soul climbs the High Way,

And the Low Soul gropes the Low,

And in between, on the misty flats,

The rest drift to and fro.

But to every man there openeth

A High Way, and a Low,

And every man decideth

The Way his soul shall go.

John Oxenham

Selected Poems of John Oxenham

Listen….

Then the disciples asked Him, saying "What does this parable mean?" And He said, "To you it has been given to know the mysteries of the kingdom of God, but to the rest it is given in parables. That, "Seeing they may not see and hearing they may not understand. Now the parable is this: The seed is the word of God." The sower sows the word.

REMEMBER. REMEMBER. REMEMBER.

Printed in the United States
1399900002BC/16-18